BATMAN v SUPERMAN.
DAWN OF JUSTICE

D0013243

BATMAN v SUPERMAN

DAWN OF JUSTICE

Cross Fire
Written by Michael Kogge

Inspired by the film *Batman v Superman:
Dawn of Justice*
Written by Chris Terrio and David S. Goyer

Batman created by Bob Kane with Bill Finger

Superman created by Jerry Siegel and Joe Shuster
By special arrangement with the Jerry Siegel family

Scholastic Inc.

All rights reserved. Published by Scholastic Inc., *Publishers since 1920.* SCHOLASTIC and associated logos are trademarks and/or registered trademarks of Scholastic Inc.

The publisher does not have any control over and does not assume any responsibility for author or third-party websites or their content.

No part of this publication may be reproduced, stored in a retrieval system, or transmitted in any form or by any means, electronic, mechanical, photocopying, recording, or otherwise, without written permission of the publisher. For information regarding permission, write to Scholastic Inc., Attention: Permissions Department, 557 Broadway, New York, NY 10012.

This book is a work of fiction. Names, characters, places, and incidents are either the product of the author's imagination or are used fictitiously, and any resemblance to actual persons, living or dead, business establishments, events, or locales is entirely coincidental.

ISBN 978-0-545-91630-1

10 9 8 7 6 5 4 3 2 1   16 17 18 19 20
Printed in the U.S.A.   40
First printing 2016
Book design by Rick DeMonico

*To ordinary kids whose little acts of justice
make them everyday Super Heroes*

PROLOGUE

When the lights switched off inside Doctor Babrius Aesop's padded cell, he didn't waste his time wondering what had caused the power outage. He went right into action.

He tried the door first, but it remained locked, as he thought it would be. A secondary system controlled the doors just in case of an outage like this. What the architects of the Arkham Asylum for the Criminally Insane hadn't planned for was that someone of Aesop's engineering skill could subvert this secondary system.

Aesop stood on the cot that was bolted to the ground. Reaching up, he unscrewed the light fixture on the ceiling and pried loose its socket, exposing a tangled mess of red and black wires.

Aesop smiled. *Perfect.*

Carefully, he twisted the wires around each other, then hopped off the cot.

He inserted both ends of his wire twist into the thin gap between the door lock and the jamb. Sparks flew, then there was a *click*. Aesop tried the door again. This time, it opened.

The power outage had triggered the emergency alarms. Aesop used the strobing lights to find his way down the dark corridor. He passed cells where the inmates shouted, banging against their doors. In another cell he heard maniacal laughter. Aesop declined to help. Better these lunatics and jokers stay locked up here. He didn't want their competition after he got out.

One cell he did unlock. The inmate who ran out nearly poked Aesop with his antlers he was so excited. "Thank you, thank you! Jack will work extra hard for you, extra hard!"

"Shut that big mouth of yours, Jackalope," Aesop snarled. "You're louder than the alarms!"

"Sorry, Doctor Aesop, sorry," Jackalope said. The short man had gotten his name because he resembled a jackrabbit with antelope horns. Bad genes cursed him with floppy ears, a button nose, and buck teeth. But his antlers were a personal choice. He wore the heavy horns on a headband that was fastened underneath his jaw. He refused to take them off, and any attempts by doctors to remove them triggered a screaming fit that could last for days. Jackalope was, like many of the patients at Arkham, truly crazy—and for the moment, also useful.

"Follow me," Aesop said.

He took Jackalope into the warren of offices

where the psychologists wrote their reports on their patients. Since it was after hours, they had all gone home for the day. And the guards who usually were stationed here had left to deal with the fried generator.

Aesop grabbed a white lab coat from the closet and slipped into it. Searching the desks, he found a pair of glasses with broken frames. He popped out the lenses, taped the frames, and put them on. With a pair of scissors, he chopped off his shoulder length hair and as much as he could of his shaggy beard. He turned to Jackalope. "How do I look?"

Jackalope squinted. "Where did Doctor Aesop go?"

Aesop smiled. It wasn't a great disguise, but if he stayed in the shadows, the guards at the entrance wouldn't recognize him. "It's still me, but *shhh*, you can't tell anyone if you want to go free."

Jackalope shook his antlers. "No, no, no. Won't squeal or snort. Promise."

"Good," Aesop said. "Now I'm going to need your strength."

Appealing to his positive attributes got Jackalope excited. He started to bounce from one leg to another. "Yes, yes, Jack is strong. Very strong!"

"Which is why I thought you could open those doors." Aesop pointed at a set of metal doors. This was one of the few exits that wasn't connected to the secondary security system. A thick chain and padlock did the job.

Jackalope's eyes lit up. He started to scuff his feet on the linoleum floor. "Yes, yes, Jack will open it for you!"

"Just give the padlock a yank and—"

Jackalope didn't listen to his suggestion. He was already leaping toward the door, his antlers lowered in front of him. Sharp and solid, they pierced through the metal. Jackalope then stepped back, wrenching one of the doors out of its frame. He jiggled his head and freed his antlers. The door remained standing, with the padlock chaining it to the other door, but there was a gap between them.

"Well done," Aesop said.

Jackalope grinned with pride and started to

twirl. Aesop blocked him. "Let's save the celebration until after we get out of here."

Aesop squeezed through the gap between the doors into the corridor beyond. Jackalope had a harder time because of his antlers. His bulky headgear was caught between the doors, and, for a moment, Aesop considered leaving him then and there. But the inevitable cries for help it would provoke might alert the security guards. Aesop grabbed one of Jackalope's horns and pulled him through the doors.

"Thank you, thank you, Doctor Aesop. More scrubbing and cleaning Jack will do at Gotham Gimbals factory, Jack will!"

"Quiet about that," Aesop said.

"Yes, yes, quiet, quiet," Jackalope said.

They headed down the hall toward the main lobby. Hopping along, Jackalope mumbled and grunted to himself, his version of being quiet. Aesop had to find a way to shut him up.

"You remember the stories I told you out on the yard? Remember the one about the bat and the weasel?"

"Bat and weasel—bat and weasel!"

"Then you can't make a sound so I can tell it to you."

"Please tell, Jack. Please tell. Jack won't make a sound, no sound at all."

They turned a corner, nearing the entrance to the asylum. "There once was a bat," Aesop whispered, "who was snatched by a weasel. This weasel loved the taste of birds and was ready to eat the bat. The bat squeaked that he wasn't a bird, but a mouse. For did not a bird chirp? Did it not have feathers and a beak? This weasel released the bat, since he hated the taste of mice."

"Mice, yuck," Jackalope said, with a scowl. "Yuck, yuck, yuck."

The lights started to flicker. The power was coming back on. They didn't have much time. "But the weasel's claws had injured one of the bat's wings, so the bat couldn't fly away," Aesop said, continuing to hold Jackalope's attention. "A second weasel grabbed him. This weasel loved the taste of mice and thought the bat was one. The bat chirped that he wasn't a mouse, but a bird. For didn't a mouse squeak? And what mouse had black fur and wings? This weasel released the bat, since he hated the taste of birds."

"Birds, eww," Jackalope said, his nose and eyes pinched in disgust. "Eww, eww, eww."

"Do you remember the moral of the story?" Aesop asked.

Jackalope nodded eagerly. "Always turn bad situations into good ones."

"Precisely," Aesop said.

He halted before the entry to the main lobby and barred Jackalope from going farther. Peeking around the door, he saw two guards at a desk, speaking into walkie-talkies.

Aesop leaned down to Jackalope. "The guards. Can you distract them while I open the door?"

Jackalope's nose puckered. "Those guards are never nice to Jack. So Jack will not be nice to them."

"No, don't be nice." Aesop gave him a nudge.

Jackalope sprang into the lobby and let loose a deafening howl. Reflexively, the guards dropped their walkie-talkies to cover their ears. Aesop shielded his own as he darted through the shadows, past the guards, and toward the glass doors that led to the outside.

It only took a moment for the guards to recover. As Jackalope continued to scream, one guard risked a hand off an ear to reach for her Taser. As she fired on Jackalope, Aesop slipped through the front door.

Coming outside, he breathed freedom for the first time in years. The doors clicked shut behind him. He couldn't hear Jackalope anymore. But through the glass he could see the little man had fallen to the ground. One guard threw a heavy sack over Jackalope's sharp antlers while the other hand-cuffed him tightly.

Wriggling on the floor, Jackalope looked at Aesop in desperation. Aesop shrugged and ran.

CHAPTER 1

When his alarm clock buzzed, Rory Greeley got out of bed and ready for school as he did every morning. He brushed his teeth, making sure to floss. He doused his head under the shower so he could comb down his cowlick. Sifting through his drawers, he dug out a Metropolis Metros T-shirt and pulled it over him. He wiggled his legs into a pair of skinny jeans, and then rolled on his socks. Last but not least, he packed the science project he'd been working on into his backpack, and slipped in the latest comic book issue of *Robot Force* he hadn't finished reading.

Before going downstairs, he peeked into his mother's bedroom, on the vague hope that she had come home during the night. She had not.

In the kitchen, Rory made himself a bowl of cereal and turned on the television. He had stopped watching cartoons recently in favor of MNN, the Metropolis News Network. The news anchor was interviewing the top reporter from the *Daily Planet* newspaper, Lois Lane.

"Any developments in the rescue mission?" asked the anchor.

Behind Lane lay the ruins that used to be central Metropolis. Less than two weeks ago, the unbelievable had happened. A giant, clawlike spacecraft had appeared in the sky above Metropolis. But the aliens aboard had not come in peace. Instead, they had razed a path of destruction through the city. Skyscrapers had toppled. Vast chasms had opened in the city streets. Electric grids had been demolished, causing an outage that spread all the way to Gotham.

Worst of all, people had been trapped in the rubble. On the day of the attack, Rory's mom had been downtown for a meeting at Wayne Tower. That tower was now reduced to a pile of bricks. But Rory was sure his mom was still out there—and he had a plan to find her.

"Some families can rest easy today," Lane said, "for three more survivors were dug out of the rubble last night."

Rory raised the volume on the television and leaned closer to the screen as if that would help him see better. But his mother was not among the two women and man who joined Lois Lane. He sat back, disappointed. But Lois Lane did have more good news. As more and more cell towers have come back online in Metropolis, survivors stranded in emergency shelters have been able to contact family members. It seemed like it would only be a matter of time until he answered the phone and his mom would be on the other end. But Rory wasn't just going to wait around for his mother to find him.

Rory hadn't told anyone that his mom had gone missing. He feared if he alerted the authorities, they might take him away from his home and the project he was building to find his mom. He had to pretend everything was normal.

The problem was, it wasn't. He shook the cereal box over his bowl. Only crumbs fell out. It was the last cereal box in the pantry, and he wasn't going to be able to afford another. He needed to buy an accessory for his project this afternoon with what remained of his lunch money. Food was going to have to wait until he found his mother.

On the television, the news anchor spoke over video of a man in a blue bodysuit and a red cape flying through the falling buildings. "I heard Superman was helping the rescue workers."

Lois Lane appeared in a small box. "That's right. Superman has cleared away rubble and rescued trapped civilians all over Metropolis. He's doing everything he can to help."

Rory watched as the footage cut to Superman helping pull a foreign cruise liner safely to port. "Yet if he's an alien," said the news anchor, "how is he any different from those who operated the spaceship? Can he really be trusted?"

"As a reporter, my job is to simply inform the public of the facts, not tell them who they can or can't trust," Lane said. "What I can tell you is that the mayor of Metropolis has declared his full support for Superman. He even wants a statue built to commemorate Superman's heroic efforts. You can read about it in my exclusive interview with him in today's *Daily Planet*."

"Thanks, Miss Lane," said the anchor. "And to all our viewers at home, be sure to catch the MNN telethon tonight—"

Rory switched off the television. He refused to let the report depress him. No news was good news as far as he was concerned. The rescue workers were still searching, and the shelters were full of people who still hadn't been able to call home. He was sure his mother was still out there. And when he came home today, he would finish his project and start his own search.

Slinging his book bag over his shoulder, Rory went out the side door and locked it behind him. He hid the key in the hollow of the oak tree in their yard, catching a glimpse through the branches of what looked like a man flying in the sky.

When he moved out from under the tree and looked up, he saw only clouds.

In a vast underground cave, its entrance hidden by a waterfall, Bruce leaned back in his chair, exhausted. Crime was much on his mind. He had just returned from a busy night patrolling Gotham City's streets. Though he'd been stopping criminals for the last twenty years, the streets had never had been so bad as they had been within the last two weeks. Crime had quadrupled since the so-called alien invasion.

But aliens weren't what concerned Bruce. What concerned him were the criminals from Metropolis who had moved to Gotham City. He didn't know how he could stop them all. He felt like one man against an army. Fighting the kind of war that never ended in victory.

Alfred, his family's longtime confidant and Bruce's lone friend, took the elevator into the cave. He brought with him a freshly pressed tuxedo on a hanger. "Time to get dressed in your other suit," he said in his upper-class British accent.

"I've attended too many galas this month. I can't do another one," Bruce said. His body ached from a particularly difficult fight with one of the robbers. He was getting older.

"This one's a must," Alfred said.

"Museum or library?"

"Those are next month. This is the MNN telethon for the victims of the attack."

Bruce felt ashamed for complaining. He'd lost people when Wayne Tower in Metropolis had fallen. He almost hadn't survived himself.

"How much do you think I'll bring in?" Wayne asked.

"I wouldn't be surprised if you broke someone's bank," Alfred said. "From what I hear, there are more than a few real estate developers who are eager for a private meeting with the president of Wayne Enterprises. There are rumors they want to build fancy condominiums where Wayne Tower once stood."

"How awful. They should know better than to capitalize on this tragedy," Wayne said. "They should be donating money to help the survivors, not trying to score a deal with me."

"If the world worked that way, Master Wayne, then there wouldn't be a need for Batman."

Bruce bandaged the cuts from his night's work and put on his tuxedo. Alfred folded his pocket square and tucked it into his jacket. "Very sharp, Master Wayne. Very sharp indeed."

Bruce looked at himself in the mirror. He preferred his other suit. If he wore that, he could give these greedy businessmen a real run for their money.

CHAPTER 2

It was just another typical day at Lewis Wilson Middle School. Rory met up with Ajay and his buddies before first period, read his comic book after he finished his math quiz early, and did what he had done ever since his mom hadn't come home—he pretended everything was normal. It wasn't hard when all the other kids were pretending. It had only taken a couple of days before everyone at school had gone back to their cliques and stupid jokes and bullying on the PE field. It was as if Metropolis hadn't been attacked by aliens at all.

Then again, none of them had a missing parent.

There were distractions that helped get his mind off his mom. In history, Ellie sat two seats in front of him. She had long brown hair and wore thin black glasses and was a whiz in math, too. She seemed to Rory to be exactly as the glittery letters on her T-shirt read: #Fabulous. Whenever she turned, he put on a smile. She smiled, but it was never to him. In fact, she didn't seem to notice Rory. Her friend Mina sat between them and whenever the teacher turned his back, the two girls were always showing each other photos of Superman on their phones.

Sitting across, Ajay rolled his eyes. He had a crush on Mina. "All they want to do is talk about Superman," he whispered to Rory. "I bet he's not even that good-looking. Why else wouldn't he let himself get photographed?"

Rory nodded. "What's so great about Superman?"

This man in the cape and tights was every-where—on the Internet, the news, and in the daydreams of middle school girls. Yet if Superman was as amazing as everyone said he was, why couldn't he have stopped the aliens from demolish-ing Metropolis in the first place? Why couldn't he find and rescue Rory's mom?

"Rory, what was that about Superman?" the his-tory teacher asked.

All the kids in the class looked at Rory, even Ellie. He sank in his seat, embarrassed. "Nothing, Mister Turner." He didn't say another word for the rest of the class.

Clark Kent joined Lois Lane and the other reporters in a conference room for their daily meeting with Perry White, the editor of the *Daily Planet*. Being the most recent hire at the newspaper, Clark stayed quiet while everyone else pitched stories.

Lois went first, putting forward an idea to do a "day in the life" feature on a rescue worker. White approved it straightaway and praised her morn-ing appearance on MNN. Going around the table, he approved most of the other pitches if they dealt with the alien attack on Metropolis, since those headlines were selling newspapers. For the ideas he nixed, he assigned reporters stories from a list on a whiteboard.

Finally, he turned to Clark. "Got anything for me today, Kent?"

Clark leaned forward in his chair. He had already pitched his idea to Lois, so he spoke confidently, knowing the other reporters were judging to see if he belonged in their ranks. "After the attack, there's been a mass exodus of people leaving Metropolis. Not just business owners, but also the criminal element, according to police reports. This has led to a huge spike in organized crime in Gotham City. I'd like to do a series of articles investigating who and what—"

White cut him off. "Absolutely not."

Clark pushed up his Coke-bottle glasses. "I'm sorry, I thought you wanted us to cover the attack and its repercussions."

"Our readers live in Metropolis and we write for them. What you pitched is a Gotham City story."

"But the criminals are from Metro—" Clark shut up after Lois kicked him under the table.

White stopped pacing. "You want to work for the *Gotham Free Press*, Kent, go right ahead. Heaven knows they could use the help. But while you're on my payroll, you write stories I want." He looked at the whiteboard. One assignment remained. "You're covering the MNN telethon for the victims' families."

Clark also checked the whiteboard. The assignment wasn't even slotted for newspaper publication. "It's for the website's blog?"

"When you show me your name's worthy of ink, I'll give you the ink, Kent. Right now, you're doing digital. Meeting's dismissed."

The reporters all went their different ways. Lois Lane was the first out. Clark stashed his notepad in his shirt pocket and ran after her.

"Lois—Lois!" He caught up with her in the hallway. "I don't understand. You told me it was a good pitch."

"I told you it was interesting."

"And it is. It has everything to do with

Metropolis. When crime comes back—and it will, you know it will, Lois—it'll be worse than ever. This deserves to be in the paper."

"Then that's how you should have pitched it," Lois said. "If it deserves to be in the paper, you have to prove it to Perry. You've got to be resourceful."

She turned into her office. Clark followed her. "Can't you say something to him?"

Lois shook her head. "That's not how it works here. You've got to learn the system like everyone else." She went to her desk and packed her voice recorder into a shoulder bag.

Clark sighed. "I'm just no good at pitching."

"Can't be good at everything." She grabbed her coat and walked to the door, having to nudge Clark aside to close it. "But if you want to compare notes, I'm free for a late-night pizza."

Clark blinked. Pizza was the last thing on his mind. "Ah, sure. How about Giuseppe's?"

She gave him a small smile. "Perfect. See you at eleven thirty. Sharp."

An elevator chimed and opened. Lois rushed to it, getting inside before the doors closed. For a moment, Clark's X-ray vision allowed him to see her behind the metal doors. She was still smiling. And so was he. Then the elevator descended.

"Why in the sweet blazes are you standing there, Kent? You have a deadline!"

Clark turned. Perry White glared at him from his office.

"On it, sir."

Clark took the next elevator down. If Perry wanted him to do digital, he'd do digital. He'd write Perry the best story about a telethon he'd ever read.

At lunch in the cafeteria, Rory borrowed a handful of carrots and chips off his friends. It wasn't much, but it would tide his hunger over for a few hours.

"Mommy didn't pack yours today, eh?" taunted a big kid they all called Haus.

"Forgot it at home," Rory said.

"But you *buy* your lunch every day, Rory," Ajay said.

"That's what I meant," Rory said.

Ajay sensed how uncomfortable Rory was and tried to change the subject. "So who do you guys think could win in a one-on-one matchup, Superman or Batman?"

He was referring to the mysterious vigilante who had fought crime in Metropolis's twin city for decades. It was a question that hardly needed to be asked at this table. Everyone said Superman, even Ajay. Yet Rory stayed quiet on the subject. Haus leered at him. "Don't tell me you actually like the guy who dresses up in a bat costume?"

"I didn't say that," Rory said.

"Batman's from *Gotham City*," said Smitty, another kid at their table. If you lived in Metropolis, anything from nearby rival Gotham City was *not* cool, especially their sports teams.

"I know he's from Gotham," Rory snapped back. "I just don't know who would win in a fight."

"They say Superman is as strong as a loco-motive. And his body's made of steel," Haus said, puffing out his own chest, as if it could compare to Superman.

"But maybe Rory has a point," said Ajay. "Batman's tricky, and he has all sorts of gadgets and technology. He could build something to defeat Superman."

Smitty laughed so hard his milk nearly came out of his nose. He had to wipe his face before he spoke. "Not even that starship could stop Superman. Batman can't touch him."

"That's not what I'm getting at," Rory said. "Why would they even fight? They're good guys . . . or they're supposed to be."

"Good guys have to fight, 'cause otherwise no one knows who's number one," said Haus. "Don't you read comics?"

Rory wanted to tell Haus to back off, that he knew comics better than anyone at this school. He'd been reading them since he was four. Instead, Rory did what he always did when confronted by a bully. He kept quiet.

The bell rang, and the cafeteria became pandemonium as kids scampered off to class. Rory usually was one of the first in Miss Paiva's room, since science was his favorite subject. Today he took his time, walking with Ajay.

"Something up with you?" his best friend asked.

"No. Why?"

"You just seem out of it," Ajay said.

"Haven't been sleeping well, that's all. Hard to after an alien invasion."

Ajay laughed. "You sure they were aliens? My mom thinks it's a government cover-up."

Rory shrugged and faked a smile. "You never know."

For lab partners in science, Miss Paiva chose names out of a hat. Rory detested random selection. Given his current luck, he'd be paired with Haus.

"Rory," Miss Paiva said, "you're going to be working with Ellie for this project."

Rory almost didn't believe it when he heard it. He felt like he'd won the lottery. Then he heard Mina giggling. He couldn't see Ellie, but he could guess she was mortified.

Then Mina stopped giggling when Miss Paiva picked Ajay to be her partner.

They all went to their assigned lab tables. "Hi, Rory," Ellie said. She didn't seem disappointed at all.

"Hi," he said. He had so much more to say but that was the only word that came out.

After reviewing the lesson on the board with her laser pointer, Miss Paiva requested they take out the robot designs assigned for homework so she could check them. The best robot she would use as the school's entry into the annual Metropolis-Gotham City Young Engineers' Challenge.

Rory watched the competition every year on MNN and had always dreamed of being a part of it. Ellie's design wasn't going to get them there, however. Hers was a portrait of a metal puppy colored in crayon and stickered with hearts.

"What do you think?" she asked Rory.

"It's . . . good," Rory said. But he couldn't hide his surprise. Ellie was so good at math he'd expected she'd come up with something more sophisticated than a drawing of a dog.

"I think it's awesome," said Jaden, who was at their table with his lab partner. As captain of the soccer team, he was one of the most popular kids in class.

"Thanks," Ellie said, smiling back at Jaden.

Miss Paiva didn't share Jaden's opinion when she came around. "Nice artwork, but I fail to see the design elements. How are you going to build your robot dog?"

It was the same question Rory had. To Ellie's credit, she never wavered in her answer. "I plan to use paper towel tubes for the legs and neck, a jewelry case for the head, and a shoebox for the body."

"That's a good start," Miss Paiva said. "But how does it move?"

"Move?" Ellie asked, surprised. "This is just a preliminary design, I didn't, er, plan, um . . ." She trailed off, looking embarrassed.

Rory had a solution. "There's plenty of empty space inside the shoebox and the tubes. We could add some gears, maybe a simple pulley system, and could operate it with a remote control. Maybe even add a cheap MP3 player and speaker to make it bark," Rory said.

Both Ellie and Miss Paiva stared at him. His explanation came out so quickly, he hadn't even realized he was talking. "Sorry, I didn't mean to interrupt."

"You did exactly what you're supposed to do by helping your partner out," Miss Paiva said. "Where's your design?"

"Oh yeah." Rory pulled out a plastic pencil case from his book bag. Four holes had been drilled into each corner, and a camera lens stuck out from one end. "I still need to get spinner blades so it can hover, and its central processor isn't completely programmed, but the webcam works in black and white."

Miss Paiva opened the pencil box to find a circuit board wired to a camera, a microphone, and other assorted components. "You put this together yourself?"

"I bought the parts at an electronics store, but the design is mine." Rory opened his notebook for her to see. It was full of squiggles and sketches. Ellie also leaned over to look, her eyes wide under her glasses.

"This is quite . . . incredible, Rory," Miss Paiva said. A circle of blue LED lights on the side of the case blinked in pattern. "Is that Morse code?"

"It's how he communicates," Rory said. "Voice

simulation was too expensive. Plus, even the LED drains the battery really quickly."

Ellie took a closer look at the blinking light. "I bet we could wire some solar paneling on here to increase the battery life exponentially."

The whole class was quiet. Everyone was watching Rory and Ellie bounce ideas off each other. Ellie took another look at the LED. "What's it saying?" Ellie asked.

Rory blushed. "It's a . . . preprogrammed test pattern. Doesn't mean anything."

Miss Paiva turned the pencil case around to inspect everything. "Well done, you two. I can see this partnership is going to work out well." She handed the case back to Rory then went over to the next group. The class resumed its chatter, as if nothing had happened.

Except that something had happened. Ellie was staring at his robot. "Does he have a name?" she asked.

"Not really. I hadn't even thought of that."

"How about Arr-Eee-One?" she suggested.

It took Rory a second to translate RE-1 in his head. "Is that our . . . initials?"

"We're partners, aren't we?"

"Yeah, we are," Rory said.

After a smile, she resumed talking to Jaden, but for once, Rory didn't care.

CHAPTER 3

Rory swore that he had locked the side door to the house before he left for school. But when he returned home, the door was wide open. He left his bike in the garden patch and ran inside.

"Mom! . . . Mom?"

No one answered. He checked the kitchen, the family room, even the basement. Upstairs was also empty. Had they been robbed? It didn't appear so. The TV, computer, and game console were still there. His mother's jewelry rack seemed untouched. The only other thing of great value they had was his mom's car, which should still be in the garage. She only drove it when she worked at the laboratory. If she had to go downtown, she took the train.

Just in case, Rory looked in the garage. The car was there, as was a figure in a white lab coat, sifting through the dusty file cabinets stored in the back.

"Mom?" Rory called.

The figure jumped and turned. It wasn't his mother—it was her brother, Doctor Babrius Aesop. Uncle Aesop (Rory had always called him by his last name, because five-year-old Rory could never pronounce "Babrius") looked frazzled in a bad hair-cut and taped-up eyeglasses, but he was smiling nonetheless. "Hello, Rory."

Startled, Rory didn't move from the top step of the garage. He hadn't seen his uncle for years. After his parents were divorced, Uncle Aesop had been the one who took Rory to Super Hero movies, the comic book shop, and Metros' games. Then he had inexplicably left, never to come back. His sudden disappearance had been so painful for Rory that he still hadn't gotten over it.

"I know, it's long time no see, but it's good to be home, finally. Real good." Aesop chuckled, in a way that made Rory feel uneasy. "Where's your mother?"

"She was in Metropolis during the attack," Rory said.

"Attack?"

"You know, from the alien spaceship."

Aesop blinked more than once. "Right. The attack."

"I think she's still trapped in the rubble or in one of the shelters downtown," Rory said.

Uncle Aesop scratched the scrub of his beard. "Have you told anyone?"

Rory shook his head. "On the TV they showed some kids who had lost their parents being moved away . . . I don't want that to happen."

"Smart," his uncle said, shutting the top drawer of the filing cabinet.

His mom had refused to tell Rory why Uncle Aesop had vanished. His disappearance had seemed to upset her, too. Whatever the reason, it didn't matter now. Rory had someone in his life he could trust. He began to feel hopeful. If his uncle could return, so could his mom.

"You'll help me find her, won't you?"

"Yes, of course I will, of course." His uncle came toward Rory, grinning again. "Why else do you think I'm here?"

Rory let out a sigh of relief. "I'm so glad you came back. It's . . . it's hard doing this all alone."

Uncle Aesop patted his shoulder. "We'll find her, don't you worry."

"I can show you what I've been building—"

"Later," his uncle said. "The best thing right now would be to check my sister's more recent files, those pertaining to her work. They'll help me track her possible whereabouts. Might you know where she would have them?"

"Maybe on her computer? She keeps everything electronically now."

"I'd like to see it," Uncle Aesop said.

Rory took him upstairs, into his mother's bedroom where she had her laptop. But a search of the files on her hard drive did not uncover what his uncle wanted. "Could they be somewhere else? These work files would be very important, so she might keep them in a secret location."

Rory thought about it for a moment. "There is one last place."

In her closet, Rory pushed back some dresses on the rack, revealing a small locked safe. "That's it. It must be," his uncle said. "You know where the key is?"

"Probably on Mom's key ring. Let me see if I can find it."

Rory checked the hook in the garage. He rummaged through the kitchen drawers. He went through his mom's desk. He even looked under the flowerpots and the laundry room mat. He found nothing.

"Sorry," he told his uncle in the kitchen. "We could try a paper clip."

"A paper clip? Are you kidding me?" Uncle Aesop's smile was gone. "This isn't some comic book, nephew."

"It was just a suggestion," Rory said.

The phone rang. His uncle grabbed it and answered. "Yes, hello. No, his mother isn't around. This is his uncle." He eyed Rory, who stood a couple of feet away. "He did? Interesting. I can sign the permission slip, yes. I agree, it would be good for him. Nice to talk to you, too."

Uncle Aesop hung up. "That was your teacher, Misses Pay—"

"Miss Paiva?"

"She wants to enter your project in some engineering contest."

"Really?" Rory suddenly imagined Ellie and him at the Metropolis-Gotham City Young Engineers' Challenge. They would be on TV together, they would be famous—

His uncle interrupted that dream. "Why didn't you tell me you built a robot?"

"I did," Rory said. "I was going to show it to you before we started to look for Mom's files."

"Show it to me now," his uncle commanded.

Rory unzipped his backpack and pulled out the pencil case. "I call him Arr-Eee-One."

His uncle snorted, took the case from him, and opened it. He examined the circuits inside. "Simple . . . but an efficient wiring pattern."

"Shortest current means fastest speed," Rory said.

"Did you design this for flight?"

"That's why I made it so light," Rory said. "I was planning to buy the spinner blades from the electronics store today. Once I install those, my unit will be better than the drones you can buy off the Internet."

His uncle seemed more and more intrigued. "What's the quality of the webcam?"

"High-definition resolution that can be streamed over any wireless connection."

Uncle Aesop noticed the blinking LEDs. "And it communicates in Morse code."

Rory was pleased his uncle had noticed. "I'd like to add voice processing and recognition, but that'll need a faster processor. I ran out of money in the cookie jar to buy one, and was considering maybe taking up a paper route—"

"The cookie jar?" His uncle swept his gaze around the kitchen.

"Yeah, I'll show you."

Hoping his uncle would spring some cash for the processor, Rory took out the cookie jar from the lazy Susan. He opened it, showing it held no bills or cookies. But something small inside rattled. "Might not have got the last penny."

His uncle reached into the jar and removed not a penny, but a small key.

"I didn't even think of looking there," Rory said.

Uncle Aesop hurried upstairs. Rory followed. The key unlocked the safe in his mother's closet, from which his uncle withdrew a tiny flash drive. He rushed over to the laptop and plugged it into a side port. After a few clicks and a search of the flash drive's directories, he started to laugh. It wasn't the same laugh that Rory remembered. This laugh sounded crazy.

"You said those files would lead to my mom?" Rory asked.

Uncle Aesop turned. His wide eyes were terrifying and made Rory step back. Yet almost immediately, the madness faded from his features and he stopped laughing. He smiled, the gentle uncle once again.

"Go buy the spinners for your robot. By the time you return, I'll have looked through these files and will know where we can get a working AI processor."

"AI? As in artificial intelligence?"

"If we want to find your mother, we should have the best technology," his uncle said.

"That would be awesome!" Rory said. "If we put in an AI processor, Arr-Eee-One could operate independently, and look in places the rescue workers and Superman can't get to."

His uncle's brows knitted together. "Superman? Who's Superman?"

Rory almost burst out in a crazy laugh himself. Wherever Uncle Aesop had been all these years, he must never have turned on a television.

CHAPTER 4

Clark Kent pushed through the crowd of people that surrounded the entrance to the Hotel Grand Lux, one of the few downtown venues still standing after the attack. Stage and screen celebrities who lived in Metropolis, along with a few from Gotham City, walked down the hotel's red carpet, waving and shaking the hands of their screaming fans. Although

Clark could have moved past them all with super-speed, he didn't let frustration get the better of him. Instead, he nudged and elbowed his way forward like a regular human being.

A policewoman stopped him at the hotel door. "You need to step back, sir."

"I'm press." Clark showed his credentials on his lanyard.

"Enter over there." She pointed to a side door, where a line of people waited. None looked like professional reporters. One had a GoPro camera on her head, another was somehow typing into a cell phone and a tablet at the same time, while a third was wearing an indie band T-shirt under a suit coat.

"Ma'am, I'm from the *Daily Planet*, not a website run out of someone's basement."

"Press is press," the policewoman said.

Clark sighed and walked over to the line, right behind the webcam man and a student from a high school newspaper. Though his superpowered hearing didn't extend all the way to the Daily Planet Building, he could only guess Perry White was laughing in his office. This must be White's form of initiation.

As demoralizing as it was to be considered just another blogger, Clark couldn't let it discourage him. A good reporter should be able to find a story wherever he was. He would prove to White that he could do it here.

Clark listened.

He tuned his super-hearing to the red carpet and the crowd. Most of what was said revolved around how pretty or handsome a celebrity was, or what new project he or she was doing, or how a fan promised never to wash her hands after shaking the hand of Bruce Wayne. More interesting was the conversation around him, between the bloggers in line.

"I hope Superman comes," the man in the T-shirt said. He was talking to the woman with the GoPro. "I'd like to give the freak a solid one-two in the chin and tell him and his ilk to fly back to Krypton, or whatever secret government lab they came from."

"Now that'd be a photo! Hashtag it Batman fights Superman and you'll get thousands of clicks to your site," the woman said, while clicking links on her phone.

"You betcha," the man said. "Then everyone can read about the bad things that have happened in Gotham City since Superman showed up. Like the cover-up at Arkham Asylum. You know that Doctor Aesop escaped?"

"No. Who's he?" the woman asked.

Finishing his shake, the man crushed the cup in his hand. "Ex-engineer who worked in the robotics division of WayneTech. He was institutionalized for some kind of delusional behavior, like wanting to take over the world or something."

The woman laughed. "Who doesn't?"

"Well, now he's loose, along with a bunch of the other criminals that are ransacking Gotham City. Check it out on my site." The man dug out a business card and handed it to the woman.

Clark stepped toward them. "Might I have one, too?"

The man eyed Clark's badge. "*Daily Planet*? When did you guys ever cover events like this?"

"We're . . . trying to reach a new audience," Clark said.

The hotel opened the side door and the line started to file inside. The man in the T-shirt gave Clark his card. "My advice, stop putting Superman on your front page. He gets too much free press. Investigate what's really going on. Find out who he really is."

"I'll tell my editor," Clark said.

The cop guarding the hotel entrance gestured for the bloggers to keep moving inside. The man in the T-shirt waved awkwardly and walked into the hotel. Clark stayed behind and typed the card's website address into his phone. The site was slow to load, but he was lucky to be near one of the working cell towers.

"You coming? 'Cause I've got to shut this," the cop said.

The site finally appeared on Clark's phone— and what he read startled him.

"Thanks, but I've got another story to cover," he said.

Clark hurried away from the hotel, and found somewhere private to change.

Within moments, Clark Kent became Superman. Leaping upward, he soared into the sky and flew across the bay to Gotham City.

The spinner blades and solar panel Rory bought from the electronics store worked like a charm. The blades provided RE-1 the maneuverability to dart through the rooms of the house, and gave the robot the lift to fly over the roof. And the solar panel helped the battery last much, much longer—just like Ellie had hoped.

But even with these improvements, his uncle wouldn't call RE-1 a robot. He called it a drone. "It won't be a robot until we can acquire the AI processor."

Rory used his remote control to land RE-1 on the kitchen table where his uncle was working on the laptop. It skidded across the wood, pushing place mats off the edge. He was glad his mom couldn't see. She would have a fit.

He picked the place mats up and put them back. "You said you were going to find a processor?"

"I have." His uncle turned his mom's laptop around so Rory could see. The screen showed an architectural diagram of a building.

"What's that?" Rory asked.

"WayneTech headquarters."

Rory found the diagram difficult to read, but he recognized the layout. He had been there a couple of times for holiday parties. "Mom works there when she doesn't have to go downtown for meetings."

"And that's where the AI processor is." His uncle pointed out a rectangular room. "In this laboratory."

Rory was confused. "I thought you were going to look on the Internet or something for sellers. Mom's lab is top secret. They won't let us have any of the equipment there."

"Which is why we're going to have to take it," Uncle Aesop said calmly.

"Take it? You mean, like *steal* it?"

His uncle frowned when Rory said that word.

"It's not stealing when the person taking it is the person who invented it."

Rory looked at the diagram on the laptop, then at his uncle. "I didn't know you work for WayneTech. Mom never said anything."

Uncle Aesop's right leg trembled. His upper lip convulsed. "Your mom didn't tell you everything. She was watching over my . . . *invention* when I went away for a while. Since I have returned, I have come to reacquire it."

Rory tugged nervously on his T-shirt. He didn't like where this conversation was going. "Are you sure we can't buy something like it on the Internet? Things have changed since you left, Uncle Aesop. Technology's gotten much better. They even do same-day shipping."

His uncle glared at him. "Do you want to find your mother or not?"

Now Rory was getting angry. "Yes—that's all I want."

"Then we should use the best," his uncle said. He drummed his fingers on RE-1's case. "Our drone needs this processor."

Rory gripped the other side of the case. "But how are we going to take it? Do you still have your badge to get in?"

"My badge? *My badge?*" Uncle Aesop erupted into laughter. "No, nephew. You're going to go get it for me."

Rory swallowed. *"Me?"*

A crazy smile accompanied his uncle's crazy laugh. "Let me tell you a story about the fish and the fisherman . . ."

Bruce Wayne mingled with the high rollers and celebs in the lobby of the Hotel Grand Lux. He loathed crowds, but at least with the people outside, all they wanted were friendly handshakes and autographs. Those who could afford to be in the hotel lobby sought the same, except that Bruce's handshakes would close their business deals and his autographs would endorse their checks. Bruce declined them all, with a polite smile and a clink of his champagne glass. When the lights dimmed, Bruce gave his unfinished drink to a waiter and hurried toward the banquet hall.

"Mister Wayne," a female voice said behind him. "Might you have a moment?"

Bruce glanced back. A tall woman in a dark blouse and matching glasses approached. "Sorry," Bruce said, "they're going to auction me onstage at any moment."

"Same for me—we can walk together," called out a young man who hurried past the woman. His stringy brown hair was parted in the middle and fell to the shoulders of his oversized corduroy jacket.

Bruce bristled at the sight of Lex Luthor.

Despite his eccentricities and slovenly appearance, the ambitious young CEO had turned his company, LexCorp, into one of Wayne Industries' main rivals in the technology sector.

"How are you, Bruce? I've been worried," Lex asked, his smile disingenuous.

"As you can imagine, I've been better."

"The collapse of Wayne Tower was a tragedy. I cried when I saw it happen on television, didn't I, Miss Graves?"

Lex's much better dressed assistant nodded. "You said it'd be tough for Mister Wayne to recover."

"Very tough," Lex said. "To think of all the cutting-edge technology that went down with it . . ."

Bruce halted, insulted. "What's tough is that I can never recover the people I lost."

Lex blinked. "That's what I was referring to. We can't do this all alone, can we?"

Bruce grunted and power-walked into the banquet hall.

"If you need my help, Bruce, don't hesitate to ask," the young man shouted out to him.

Not in a million years would Bruce Wayne ever do that. He'd rather strike a deal with a condo developer than beg Lex Luthor for money.

After the ticketed crowd had been seated at the tables, the MNN anchor reviewed the rules of the telethon, saying that there would be a fifteen-minute auction for every guest. Bids could be announced in the hall or called in via telephone from viewers at home. The winner would be treated to an hour-and-a-half hotel lunch meeting with the guest they bid on. All monies would help victims and families who suffered because of the alien attack.

Bruce was set to be bid on in the middle of the pack. Behind the stage curtains, he stood in the corner, ignoring Luthor and the others. Right before he was about to go out, his phone buzzed. He saw who was calling and picked up.

"Don't tell me you're going to make a bid, Alfred?"

"Would you like me to, Master Wayne? It has been a while since the two of us had lunch together," Alfred said over the phone.

"When the crime in Gotham City drops, I'll take you," Bruce said.

"That's why I'm calling, Master Wayne. I regret to inform you that there's been a break-in at WayneTech."

"Any idea of the culprit?"

"None. The alarms were tripped in the ventilation shafts, where there aren't cameras installed."

The news anchor dipped his head through the curtains. "Mister Wayne, they're ready for you."

"Get my other suit prepped, Alfred. I'll be there soon." He clicked off the call and looked at the news anchor. "I apologize, but you're going to have to do the auction without me."

"Without you? You're one of the main attractions!"

Bruce started toward an emergency exit. "Then make it a two-hour lunch. And say I'll even listen to a business proposal, if that'll help raise more money." He glanced at Lex Luthor, who was holding court with some of Metropolis's movers and shakers. "In fact, whatever Luthor is offering, double it."

Once outside, Bruce walked past the crowds peeking into the hotel windows. So focused were they in their celebrity spotting, they didn't notice when Bruce ducked into the parking garage. Only at the roar of his sports car's engine did they turn, but by that time, he was speeding off.

CHAPTER 5

There once was a fisherman who knit together the biggest, strongest net, so as to catch the biggest, strongest fish," Uncle Aesop said to Rory as they gathered supplies in the house. "Out into the choppy seas he went. Never had he seen so many schools of fish darting around his boat. He cast his net into these waters, believing he'd become a rich man for catching so many fish."

"But he didn't, did he?" Rory asked. His uncle had told him many of these kinds of stories when he was younger. They always had a moral to them.

"Don't interrupt me," Uncle Aesop said.

"Sorry." As far as Rory remembered, his uncle had never snapped at him like that when he was younger.

"When the fisherman pulled up his net," Uncle Aesop continued, "he saw he had caught only a single large tuna. The other fish, being smaller, had slipped through the holes of his net. He had thought he was going to be rich, but now he was going to be poor." He packed the laptop into a shoulder bag. "Do you know the moral of this fable?"

Rory shook his head. He didn't know and he didn't care.

"Guess," his uncle said, repeating it louder, "guess!"

Rory scooted toward the side door. He couldn't wait to get on his dirt bike, away from his uncle. "One net doesn't fit all?" he offered.

His uncle's brow furrowed. "How did you know that?"

Rory shrugged. "You asked me to guess, so I did." What he didn't say was that he probably heard the story a long time ago, but he didn't recall all the details.

"Well, you're right—one net doesn't fit all." His uncle grabbed Rory's mom's car keys from the hook.

"I don't understand," Rory said. "What's the point of that story?"

"The point is it's why you have to go, alone." His uncle opened the garage door. "The only way inside is through the ventilation shaft. I won't fit in it, but you will."

Rory found what he was about to do highly questionable, but it was hard to say no to his uncle, especially when his mom's rescue was on the line. He had to trust that Uncle Aesop knew what he was doing.

While his uncle drove to an abandoned factory in Gotham City to prepare for their search, Rory rode his dirt bike to the WayneTech building. He stayed far away from the main entrance, so as not to be caught on the security cam. Instead, he sneaked along the side wall where his uncle had located a large duct on the architectural diagram. Rory parted the weeds that covered the duct, then bent the metal slits to squeeze himself through. With RE-1 strapped to his back, he crawled forward on his hands and knees. The tunnels were dusty and made him sneeze.

A Maglite attached to the front of RE-1 provided meager illumination in what seemed like a never-ending maze of rattling aluminum. The turns were always sharp right angles, forcing Rory to contort his body. He endured cuts on his hands from slicing them on the edges. But he never let the pain slow him down. Not with what was at stake. Wherever his mom was, he would not give up on her. With the new and improved RE-1, he was sure he would find her.

When he peered through the occasional venti-lation grille, all he saw were dim hallways. Growing discouraged, he tilted his head to whisper into RE-1's microphone. "What exactly am I looking for?"

Uncle Aesop had incorporated a cell p
into the robot's componentry so it could transmit
visual and audio data over long distances. "The
engineering laboratory. Should be white and sterile
and full of sophisticated technology," his uncle
replied over the tinny speaker.

Rory kept crawling. He wished he had a map,
but his uncle said the architectural drawings didn't
show the ventilation system. All he could do was put
one hand in front of the other and drag himself
along.

He finally came to another grille. The slits were
so narrow he had to press his face against it to see
anything. From this vantage point, he noticed wiring diagrams on whiteboards and testing circuits on
long tables. Two hazmat suits hung on a rack. It had
to be the laboratory.

Rory scooted back, and then removed the vent
grille with the screwdriver tool of his four-in-one
scout knife. He could then see that it was indeed a
laboratory, with the sterile white walls that Uncle
Aesop had mentioned, along with oscilloscopes

and other instrumentation. Getting down there safely was going to be a problem, however. It was a twenty-foot drop to the floor, and there seemed to be nowhere to climb down.

"What are you waiting for? Start moving!" shouted his uncle on the speaker. The RE-1's camera lens was capturing everything for his uncle to view remotely.

"How? I could break my arm, or even my neck."

"Your mother might be enduring something far worse," Uncle Aesop said.

That was all Rory needed to keep going. His mother could be paralyzed, pinned under a rock, unable to move. Perhaps that's why no one had found her yet. It would be tough for even Superman to find someone who couldn't signal that they needed to be rescued.

Rory braced himself to jump. But he didn't make the plunge. It might not be his bones that would break, but RE-1.

He undid the straps that tied the robot to his back. His uncle had installed spinner blades that folded downward from each corner of the case. He claimed the blades could support a heavy weight, yet did not have the opportunity to test them.

That test would have to fall on Rory's shoulders.

Rory straightened the poles of each of the four spinner blades so they stood upright. Putting RE-1 on his back, he retied the straps, tighter than before. Then, after a deep breath, he switched on the spinners and dropped from the vent.

But he didn't drop. He hovered. Twenty feet over the ground. The spinner blades rotated so quickly they held Rory aloft.

He reached back to the case and pushed a button to power down a single blade. When it stopped spinning, he fell a few feet until the other blades took up the slack. How long the wheezing motors would last, he wasn't going to wait and see. He powered down a second blade, a third, and then the final one, dropping to the floor in spurts. He landed on his chest with a bone-shaking *thud*, but when he stood, all his bones, along with RE-1, were intact.

"You okay?" asked his uncle.

"Yeah," Rory said, sniffing. "All that dust irritated my allergies, though."

"If you just do what I tell you to do, you'll be out of there soon. Fix the camera so I can see the surroundings."

Rory hoisted RE-1 up on his back and swiveled the lens over his shoulder. He turned in a full circle to give his uncle a full view. "That better?"

"Aha! I knew it was here!" his uncle said.

Rory kept turning. "What? Where?"

"On the table to your right, at three o'clock—no, rotate the other way—there's the casing for an AI brain," relayed his uncle. "Open it to gain access to the motherboard. The processor's inside."

Swinging his camera with him, Rory saw tools and circuit probes cluttering the table. In the center lay a metal sphere from which wires ran out of a back panel. "Is this it?"

"Yes, yes—open it!"

Rory got out his screwdriver tool and stepped over to the sphere.

"Hello there," said a digitized voice. Two

glowing green orbs lit up on the front plate of the sphere. Rory froze.

"What are you doing? Don't stop!" his uncle said.

"It just . . . talked to me," Rory whispered.

"Of course it did—it's a real robot!"

A *real* robot. Not some radio-controlled drone, but a machine that could imitate human behavior and thinking. Could it recognize that Rory was frightened? Could it determine what he was about to do?

"It is nice to meet you," said the robot head. "Do you have a name?"

"Yeah." He approached, slowly. "Rory."

His uncle huffed over RE-1's speaker. "Don't talk to it! Just get the processor!"

"I don't have a name yet, only a designation," said the robot head. "Test unit nineteen-thirty-three."

Rory rotated the head around to unscrew the back panel. Despite what his uncle had said, he continued talking. "My friend Ellie would be sad they didn't give you a name."

"Sad?" Servos whirred inside its head. "My internal dictionary says that 'sad' is the antonym of happy. It is an emotional state when humans do not feel one hundred percent."

Rory pulled off the back panel. "That's a pretty good definition."

"Presently I am only seventy-eight percent complete." The robot's eyes dimmed to a lower setting. "So according to that definition, I am sad."

"You and me both." Rory peeked inside the robot's head. His Maglite revealed a spaghetti tangle of wires around a silicon motherboard.

"Stop blabbing and cut those wires," Uncle Aesop ordered.

Rory tilted his head toward RE-1's mic. "But if I cut them, I'll deactivate the robot."

"What's worth more to you—a robot or your mother's life?"

Alarms started to blare through the complex. Emergency lights flashed. He must've triggered something. Perhaps there were cameras inside the laboratory. He didn't have much time. Security would be here soon.

"Do it!" yelled his uncle, his voice testing the limits of RE-1's speaker. "Cut them now or you won't be able to get out!"

Rory had no choice. He popped out the blade of his scout knife, slid it underneath the tangle of wires, and sawed them apart.

The eyes on the robot head darkened. The speaker mouth went mute. Rory felt terrible. After this was all said and done, and his mother was found, he vowed to resolder the connections and revive the brain.

"Now the processor," his uncle said.

Under the cut wires, he located the square AI chip snug in its motherboard socket. It boggled his mind that something so small could pack so much computing power. Since it was too delicate to use his knife to pry it loose, he wiggled it free with his fingers.

"Put it back," said a gravelly voice that wasn't his uncle's.

Out from the shadows and flashing alarms strode a tall man. He was cowled in a black mask that revealed only his eyes and the lower part of his face.

Ridges on each side of the mask crested like savage ears. He wore matching black boots, black gloves, and a long black cape. The muscles of his chest and legs were well defined under the tight weave of his gray bodysuit. A Utility Belt laden with accessories and tools was cinched around his waist.

Emblazoned on his chest was a bat with its wings spread.

Rory gasped, out of wonder—and fear. He was looking at none other than Batman. *The* Batman.

"Get out of there!" Uncle Aesop screamed.

But Batman's stare held Rory in place. There was little chance of escape from a vigilante whom newspapers called the "Caped Crusader." He'd apprehended some of Gotham City's most infamous villains. Rory was no cunning criminal, just a kid.

"I won't repeat my request," Batman said.

Rory gulped. Barely clinging onto the chip in his trembling hands, he started to reach into the robot head to the motherboard socket.

He lost his footing on the floor.

But he didn't fall. He rose.

The spinner blades on the RE-1 had switched on, all four at once, launching him twenty feet into the air. His uncle must have issued the command remotely. Rory bopped his head on the ceiling and bounced against a wall. No sooner did he get his bearings than something came at him fast. A boomerang in the shape of a bat.

It connected with his spinner blades and stopped all four of them dead. Falling, Rory flailed out with his arms. Another Batarang whirled at him. It caught the side of his Metros tee and propelled him backward, tacking him to the wall.

Rory dangled by a stretch of T-shirt fabric, amazed by Batman's incredible aim. His precision throw had stopped Rory dead in his tracks without even grazing his arm.

"You done, kid?" Batman asked.

Rory wanted to say yes. He wanted to turn himself over to Batman. He wasn't made for missions like this. But if he did, he'd have to surrender the AI processor. Batman would undoubtedly bring him to the authorities, who would question him to no end.

The search for his mother would end before it even started.

"Sorry, Batman."

Kicking both feet against the wall, Rory launched himself at the vent, ripping his T-shirt in the process. He whacked the opposite wall with his chin, but also caught the edge of the vent. Using all his strength, he heaved himself up through the opening, and then shimmied down the shaft on all fours. A third Batarang, attached to a trip wire, clanged behind him, missing his sneakers by inches.

Worming through the ventilation ducts, Rory realized that Batman could've used more extreme measures to capture him. Despite his frightful costume and tough guy methods, the masked vigilante had a sense of honor.

Rory hoped that if Batman ever learned the truth about his mom's situation, Batman would understand that Rory was trying to act honorably, too.

Batman deactivated the building's alarms and gave himself a few minutes before he went outside. The dirt bike he'd previously seen in the weeds was gone. The boy had gotten away.

Good. Everything had gone as planned.

Batman returned to his vehicle and radioed Alfred. "Is the tracer set?"

"It deployed from your Batarang onto the boy's shirt beautifully," Alfred responded. He had remained behind in the Batcave to monitor the situation. "Sending tracking data now to the Batmobile. Tracer location will be red."

The dashboard screen displayed a top-down map of the Gotham City–Metropolis bridge. A red marker blinked in the blue area that represented the surrounding waterway.

Batman gritted his teeth. "Don't even tell me he's swimming."

"Not that deep," Alfred said. "He must have found the beacon and hurled it into the bay. Our little thief's smarter than we thought."

Indeed he was—or whoever was behind him.

"You have any idea as to his motivation?" Batman asked. That was the real question behind all of this. What twelve-year-old kid would break into a high-security laboratory and steal an advanced artificial intelligence processor? It didn't make sense. Someone must be using the boy as a tool. And that someone was the person Batman wanted to catch.

"None at the moment," Alfred said. "But did I hear the boy use the name Rory?"

"That's what he told the AI, yes," Batman said. "Do a search query on both his name and WayneTech. Maybe he's related to one of the employees."

"Commencing database search now," Alfred said. Photos of numerous employees flashed by on the dashboard screen. "This is interesting."

The screen showed the profile of one Amelia Greeley. She was a midlevel engineer at WayneTech specializing in robotics. Over her couple of years with the company, she had earned stellar performance reviews. But there was a flag on her file.

Batman grimaced. Alfred's sigh was audible over the radio.

Amelia Greeley was among those still missing after Wayne Tower collapsed.

Born on the faraway planet of Krypton, Superman uses his alien powers to fight for the people of Earth.

When Superman isn't fighting crime, he works for a newspaper called the *Daily Planet* as Clark Kent.

Clark's editor, Perry White, is always on the lookout for the next big story.

Lois Lane also works at the *Daily Planet* as an award-winning reporter.

When Clark takes to the skies as Superman, he is always ready to help people in need.

Many people look up to Superman for saving so many people.

But some people worry that Superman could be dangerous.

Batman is also a crime fighter. He has vowed to protect the people of Gotham City.

Batman is a man named Bruce Wayne, and he does not have superpowers like Superman. Instead, he uses gadgets to defeat villains.

Batman keeps one step ahead of his enemies by constantly developing new gadgets in his Batcave.

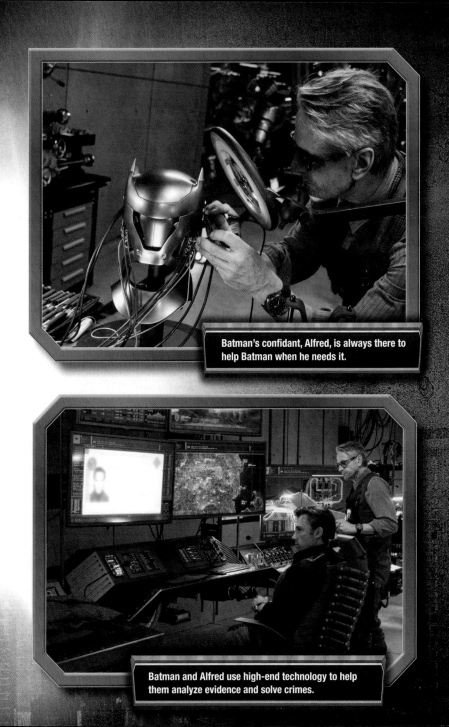

Batman's confidant, Alfred, is always there to help Batman when he needs it.

Batman and Alfred use high-end technology to help them analyze evidence and solve crimes.

The Batcave not only stores Batman's gadgets and Batsuit, but also Batman's greatest weapon against crime: the Batmobile.

With such a powerful arsenal, Batman is ready to take on any villain.

After a deep breath, Batman proceeded to click through her records. She had noted on her insurance information that she had one son, named Rory.

Still, none of this added up as to why the kid would do what he did. Retaliation for a past grievance? Revenge?

"Birth records reveal another interesting family connection," Alfred said.

A second set of records appeared on the screen. Her maiden name, before her marriage, had been Aesop.

Just seeing the name incensed Batman. "I hope she's not related to *him*."

"I'm afraid she's the mad doctor's sister," Alfred said.

Batman started the engine. Things were beginning to fall into place. The kid's uncle was none other than the former chief scientist of WayneTech, Doctor Babrius Aesop, who had been committed to Arkham Asylum for threats against humanity.

"I think we have a suspect," Batman said.

CHAPTER 6

uried in the rambling blog post about the Arkham Asylum cover-up, the rise in Gotham City criminal activity, and conspiracy theories concerning alien "Supermen" was a nugget of information that Clark felt he had to investigate. A vagrant reported seeing someone who matched Doctor Aesop's description wandering about Gotham City's seedy warehouse

district, near the old Gotham Gimbals factory. Since Arkham Asylum claimed no one had escaped, the matter had not been investigated.

Until now.

Landing behind an adjacent warehouse, Clark changed back into his reporter attire and made his way toward the abandoned factory on foot. He did not want the sight of Superman to scare off Aesop or any other potential informant. Clark knew he could get in trouble at the *Daily Planet* for missing the telethon to come here. But he was also certain all would be forgiven if he uncovered a great story, like finding an escaped criminal.

Even if he didn't find anything here, Clark could still dash off a piece about the telethon for the newspaper's website. Telethons were *televised* after all. A quick call to the *Daily Planet* offices guaranteed that the event would be recorded, for Clark's "research."

Lois would be proud at his resourcefulness. This was something she would do.

His shoes crunched on broken bottles as he approached the decrepit building. Most of its windowpanes had been long since smashed. Graffiti painted its brick front. What remained of a termite-infested door dangled from a rusty hinge. Clark pushed it open and stepped inside.

"Hello?"

He heard nothing except the squeak of the door shutting behind him. Moonlight slanted through the windows, revealing that the inside fared no better than the outside. Weeds had broken through floor tiles to flourish around workbenches. Mice squeaked from antique machinery, while an owl hooted from a roof beam. Like sprinkles of metallic stardust, stainless-steel filings covered the tables where workers assembled gimbals for use in everything from camera tripods to handheld compasses. The gimbals themselves rusted in moldy wooden crates and decomposed cardboard boxes. Clark didn't know when the factory had closed, but from the thick layer of dust on everything, he guessed many years ago.

There was a *click*, almost too faint for a normal person to hear, but not for one with the gifts of Clark Kent. He whirled and saw a figure in a white lab coat and mended eyeglasses emerge from stairs that descended below. Clark assumed the bulky object in the man's hand was a weapon of some sort given that it was pointed at Clark.

"Who are you?" the man demanded.

Clark wasn't afraid of the weapon. He was, after all, nearly invulnerable. But to disclose those powers here, right now, would reveal that he was Superman. He raised both hands. "I'm a reporter for the *Daily Planet*. I'm here requesting an interview with Doctor Babrius Aesop."

"How did you come here of all places?"

Clark shrugged. "I was just following a lead."

"Did anyone join you?"

Clark shook his head. "It's just me. No one else."

The man came closer, squinting at the badge on Clark's lanyard. "Clark Kent," the man said, chewing over his name. "Is the *Daily Planet* still the biggest newspaper in Metropolis?"

Clark nodded. "Both print and digital."

"And what's the purpose of this interview?"

It was a good question. Clark had been so focused on getting the story that he hadn't thought about his angle. "I . . . I'm interested in covering the rise in crime in Gotham City."

"I'm no criminal," the man said.

Clark's questions were working. The man had confirmed he was indeed Aesop. "I didn't mean to suggest you were, sir. Though I have heard you were being treated at Arkham—"

"That was a crime done to me!" Aesop's words echoed through the factory. He lowered his voice. "I've been *against* crime my entire life."

"Perhaps you can explain that to our readers?" Clark asked nicely.

Weapon twitching in his grasp, Doctor Aesop pondered over the request. Clark noticed there were no lenses in his frames. His beard growth was uneven and his hair had been sloppily cut. Yet his eyes possessed an intelligence Clark couldn't deny.

"Okay. You want to write about crime, I'll tell you about crime." Aesop dropped the weapon into a pocket in his lab coat, but kept his hand in that pocket.

Clark took out his notebook and pen. "Then

let's start at the beginning. I've read you were an engineer at WayneTech."

"I was the chief scientist—until they stole my designs for artificial intelligence."

"That's a serious charge," Clark said.

Aesop snarled. "It's one that everyone in Gotham City should know. Bruce Wayne and his minions should not be trusted."

Clark jotted down the quote in shorthand. "Do you have any proof?"

"Do I have proof?" Aesop laughed. "Follow me, Clark Kent."

He took Clark across the factory floor into a dark room where he turned on a portable flood lamp. It sat on a warped desk with a laptop computer, wires, and what looked like electronic instruments. He inserted a flash drive into the laptop. A few keystrokes later, Aesop turned the laptop screen toward Clark. "Here's your proof."

Clark flipped through the images of sophisticated engineering schematics.

"You're looking at the future of drone technology," Aesop said. "Nothing like the feebleminded reconnaissance craft the military uses or the package droppers that we have now. Drones that are fully autonomous. Intelligent. Able to make informed decisions and interact with human beings at conversational level."

"Incredible," Clark said.

Those intelligent eyes blazed. "Imagine the applications. Military, domestic, retail. Intelligent flying machines that could serve as everything from traffic cameras and pizza deliverers to terrorist hunters and aerial police. The people of Metropolis and Gotham City would have no need of Batman or Superman because my drones would catch the criminals faster!"

On the surface, what Aesop proposed seemed like a brilliant idea. No one would ever argue against making life more efficient and communities safer. Even Superman was looking for help in that area. But there were clear dangers in implementing technology on such a grand scale. Moreover, good reporters always followed up with tough questions.

"What would happen if a drone's circuits crossed? Or if one went rogue?" countered Clark.

"What if someone in power misused these drones for their own ends?"

His interview subject frowned. "You sound like my sister."

"Your sister?"

"She's the one who ratted me out. She's the one who had me committed to Arkham Asylum. Even after the alien attack, she still told me that my drones were dangerous. As if they couldn't have saved countless lives! She's why I was never able to implement my plan before now."

"Why?"

A sickle of a smile crept over Aesop's face. "Have you ever heard the story about the bat and the weasel?"

"Have you ever heard the story about the bat and the weasel?"

In all his years, Batman had seen few beings as pathetic as the inmate who posed that question. He paced from one wall to the other in his padded call, fluctuating between sniffing and snickering. His nose constantly twitched. His front teeth bucked out like a jackrabbit. He tilted his head side to side, swaying the two antelope antlers he wore on a band. If there was a poster child for Arkham Asylum, Jackalope was it.

"Have you heard it?" Jackalope asked again.

"You're not answering my question," Batman growled. "Where did Doctor Aesop go?"

Aesop was supposed to be here. Alfred had hacked into the inmate database, which confirmed Doctor Aesop's residency. Yet when Batman visited the cell, he found it empty. So either Aesop was housed in another cell—a near impossibility because Arkham was already past maximum occupancy—or he had escaped, and the staff was covering it up.

Batman assumed the latter. That assumption brought him into the cell of Aesop's most frequent acquaintance during recreation time, at least according to the database records.

Jackalope snarled. "Doctor Aesop . . . he tricked his friend! He betrayed Jack! He told Jack the story of the bat and the weasel, then left and didn't take Jack with him!" In a bout of anger,

Jackalope banged his antlers into the padded wall. The vinyl punctured. Bits of foam stuck to the tips of his antlers.

Batman could only imagine the teasing this creature must have endured throughout his life about his size, nose, ears, and buck teeth. He wore antlers to be something greater than the jack-rabbit he resembled, something more powerful—the mythical jackalope.

Was Batman any different by wearing his cape and cowl?

Feeling a sympathetic kinship with the inmate, Batman made his voice as calm as he could. "Yes, tell me about the bat and the weasel. I've never heard the story."

Jackalope lifted his antlers from the wall. His nose slowed its twitch. He stopped laughing and chortling. When he smiled, his buck teeth didn't look so big.

"There once was a bat who was snatched by a weasel . . ."

CHAPTER 7

There once was a bat who was snatched
by a weasel," began Uncle Aesop.

Ditching his dirt bike outside, Rory
tiptoed into the abandoned shoe factory.
He spotted Uncle Aesop in an adjoining room telling his fable to a younger, dark-haired man who
wrote down everything he said. A badge hung from

the younger man's neck with the symbol of the *Daily Planet*.

What was a reporter doing here? Rory's uncle had told him the sole purpose of them setting up their base in the factory rather than Rory's house was that it would be "off the grid." They could mount a rescue operation to save Rory's mother without running afoul of city regulations. They would be able to upgrade RE-1 with the artificial intelligence processor in the utmost secrecy.

That explanation didn't make much sense to Rory, though he didn't question it. Uncle Aesop had been right in ordering Rory to search his clothes for any tracer bugs. He had found one tiny electronic beacon stuck to his T-shirt and promptly discarded it into the bay. But if his uncle truly wanted to keep this place a secret, why was he talking to someone from the *Daily Planet*?

Rory slipped his arms out of the straps and gently put RE-1 down onto a workbench. Batman's Batarang lay caught in the tangle of spinner blade poles it had crumpled. With some forceful yanks, Rory pulled it out, careful of its edges. He straightened the poles the best he could. The blades themselves seemed undamaged. RE-1 should be able to fly again.

The object Rory had extracted was quite a souvenir. It was made of a lightweight metal and cut in the shape of a bat. Rory gripped one wing and flicked his wrist. He hadn't intended to release it, but it flew out of his hand naturally and wedged itself in a pyramid of metal cases nearby.

Rory glanced over to the men in the room. His uncle was still telling the story of the bat and the weasel to the reporter. They hadn't noticed his accidental target practice.

He walked past the workbenches to the pyramid. The thirty metal cases in its stack seemed to be nothing more than lockboxes just like the one his mom used to keep cash in at their annual garage sale. A closer look, however, revealed that every lockbox possessed a camera lens, two lights, and a speaker-microphone unit like RE-1. Similarly, four poles with spinner blades were folded down on the tops of each box. In place of the LEDs Rory had used for Morse code, a tube protruded with a small lens. It looked like a thicker version of Miss Paiva's laser pointer.

Was his uncle making copies of RE-1? Why hadn't he said anything? Rory could've offered some improvements to help speed up the search for his mother.

"Do you know the moral to the fable?" he heard his uncle ask the reporter. Their voices were getting louder. Rory wrested the Batarang free from between the cases, slipped it into his back pocket, and moved away from the pyramid. The men came into the center of the factory.

"Let me guess," the reporter said. "Don't judge a bat by its wings."

"Close," Uncle Aesop said. "More like turn every bad situation into a good one."

"And your bad situation was being committed to Arkham?"

Uncle Aesop grinned. "During which I spent every waking hour thinking about how I would punish Bruce Wayne and my rat of a sister—" Uncle Aesop paused, seeing Rory. "You're back."

Rory stepped toward them. "I didn't want to disturb you two."

The reporter held out a hand to Rory. "Clark Kent, *Daily Planet*."

"Rory Greeley, Lewis Wilson Middle School." Rory shook Clark Kent's hand. The man had an iron grip.

"This is your . . . nephew?" Clark asked Aesop.

He grunted. "Indeed it is."

Clark Kent looked honest and trustworthy to Rory, and might be someone who could help their search. "If you're at the *Daily Planet*, do you know Lois Lane?"

Clark laughed. "I do."

"Can you tell her to do a report on my mother, Amelia Greeley? She was downtown during the attack—"

"That's quite enough," interrupted Uncle Aesop, shooting a glare at Rory. "Mister Kent doesn't have time to chase trivialities."

"It's no biggie. I can ask Lois. We both got into the newspaper business to help people." Clark looked at Rory. "Is Amelia Greeley your mother?"

Rory nodded. Clark flipped pages in his note-pad. "I must have gotten this wrong, Doctor Aesop. You said you had spoken with Amelia after the attack."

Clark's statement cut through Rory like a Batarang to his soul. Did he hear that right? Uncle Aesop has seen his mother?

"You must have misheard me," his uncle corrected. "We're still looking for her. Every day we pray for her safe return." He smiled at Rory. "Isn't that right?"

Rory had nothing to say. He was stunned. Confused. He took a few steps away from his uncle.

Uncle Aesop grabbed Clark's arm. "The boy's been through a lot recently and I think it's best we don't stir up a hornet's nest, if you know what I mean. Let me escort you out."

Clark Kent glanced back at Rory as he was led through the squeaky door. Rory stood there, his heart hammering in his chest. Had his uncle really spoken with his mother? Could he not be telling Rory the whole truth? Why?

Was he hiding something?

When Uncle Aesop returned, alone, his friendly smile had vanished. "You have the chip? Hand it to me."

"N-n-not . . ." Rory stammered, looking his uncle right in the eye. The man was twice the size of Haus, and probably ten times the bully. But Rory couldn't wimp out again, not like he always did at school. He had to stand up for his mom. He had to discover what his uncle was hiding.

He summoned all his courage and steeled his voice. "Not until you tell me everything you know about my mother. And why did you call her a rat?"

"This is not a negotiation," his uncle snarled.

"You called her a rat. Why?"

"She's a rat because she told her bosses what I was planning to do."

"And what was that?"

"Give me the chip or I promise you will never see her again." He loomed over Rory, his hands balled into fists.

Rory held out an arm. "Fine. Take it. Just tell me the truth." He took the processor out of his pocket and gave it to his uncle.

Uncle Aesop's eyes widened like someone who had found pure gold. "Finally! My work is mine again. Soon the whole world will know my name—and I will have my revenge!" He held the chip under a shaft of moonlight and kissed it.

"Revenge? For what?" Rory dared.

His uncle chuckled. "Come. Let me show you something, nephew."

Rory followed Uncle Aesop over to the pyramid, where his uncle retrieved the top case. "You've proved a great inspiration, young man." His uncle set the case on a workbench and unlocked it with a key. Rory stood on his toes to see inside. The inner circuitry resembled that of RE-1, produced from cheap aftermarket parts.

"You used my design," Rory said.

"With a few improvements." His uncle rotated the chip so the bottom pins were at the proper angle, then fit the chip into the motherboard socket.

Red lights above the camera lenses illuminated. The poles atop the case unfolded and the blades revved up to spin. Soon the robot drone hovered in the air before Rory and his uncle.

"Test unit nineteen-thirty-three at your service," a voice said that sounded just like the robot from WayneTech lab.

His uncle spoke in a clear, commanding voice. "I am Doctor Babrius Aesop, your designer. You will be now known as Elite Drone One. You will obey only my orders, as encoded in your programming."

"Affirmative."

"As the first test of your abilities, I want you to fire your laser."

Rory scooted away from the drone. "Lasers? That wasn't part of my design."

"Like I said, I made some improvements." Uncle Aesop pointed across the factory floor. "Target that workbench," he instructed the drone.

A light began to build in intensity and sharpness in the lens of what looked like Miss Paiva's laser pointer. Rory knew not to stare at it because it could damage his eyes. After about ten seconds of warming up, a tightly focused beam of energy shot out from the drone's tube and drilled a hole into the workbench's legs. The bench collapsed.

Uncle Aesop clapped. "Your aim is impeccable, Elite Drone One."

"Affirmative," replied the drone.

Rory watched coils of smoke rise from the charred wood. "You're going to use that to blast the rocks that could be around my mother . . . right?"

"I'm going to use it to blast whatever stands in its path," Uncle Aesop said. "Elite Drone One, transmit the signal to activate your brothers and sisters. You will be their brain."

"Affirmative."

The drone emitted a squelch of electronic noise. Twin orange lights lit up on every case in the pyramid. On the top two cases, the poles unfolded and the spinner blades rotated. When those units flew over to the Elite Drone, the same happened for the cases stacked below. Within a minute, nine drones with orange lights hovered behind their leader.

"Behold my Drone Strike Team," Uncle Aesop said, "which is but the initial force of my drone army.

With them I will conquer both Metropolis and Gotham City."

Rory stood his ground. "I don't know what you're talking about. But I'm not going to be a part of it. I stole that chip so we could search for my mom. That's what we agreed to. Now tell me: *Where is my mother?*"

Uncle Aesop turned to his strike team. "Drone Two-Three-Eight, escort this little brat into the storage room. There he can start—and end—his search for his mommy."

"Affirmative." A drone came out of the pack and whisked toward Rory.

"Oh, and one more thing," his uncle added. "If he tries to run, blast him."

CHAPTER 8

atman gripped the torn vinyl of the padded cell. He felt like he was going crazy himself after listening to Jackalope's rambling tale. What had started out as a simple story about a bat and a weasel had turned into a sprawling, confusing epic about birds and mice, tortoises and hares, and even ants and grasshoppers.

"Is there an end to this?" Batman interjected.

Jackalope snorted. "An end? No end. Only a moral."

"So what's the moral?" Batman asked, trying to cut to the chase.

"Isn't it obvious? Always turn a good situation into a bad one," Jackalope said, bursting into laughter.

Batman knew the poor fool had reversed good and bad in the moral. But he didn't correct him. "You said Doctor Aesop told you that story?"

Jackalope stopped laughing. "Doctor Aesop," he hissed, "he is a liar, he is a cheat, he is a traitor!"

"I'm in full agreement," Batman said, "which is why I'd like to know what else he lied about."

Jackalope scuffed his feet on the floor. "He lied about Jack working for him. He lied about his plans."

"Plans for what?"

Jackalope squinted one eye at Batman. "To rule over Metropolis and Gotham City. To hurt Bruce Wayne for what he did to Jack."

"Bruce Wayne?" Ever so controlled, Batman

couldn't contain his shock. "What did Bruce Wayne do to you?"

"Bruce Wayne is a liar, he is a cheat, he is a traitor!" Jackalope screamed, stomping the floor. "Just like Bruce Wayne got rid of Doctor Aesop, Bruce Wayne got rid of Jack."

Batman looked at the short man. He didn't remember Jackalope ever being on the payroll, but he had thousands of employees. "*You* worked for Bruce Wayne?"

Jackalope began to pace again. "Jack worked for Bruce Wayne like Jack was going to work for Doctor Aesop. Jack is the best at cleaning and sweeping and scrubbing and wiping. Jack can mop floors and Jack can polish windows. Jack can change lightbulbs. But all these good things Jack does make no difference, because Jack wears these." He grabbed his antlers. "These cause Jack to be fired. These cause Jack to be forgotten. So no more WayneTech. No more Gotham Gimbals. No more!"

He banged his antlers into the wall and didn't stop. Batman withdrew to the door. He doubted he'd learn anything more from Jackalope, but perhaps he didn't need to. In his ravings, Jack had divulged a location that would be a perfect hiding spot for a criminal like Aesop.

Batman waved a keybreaker card over the lock and slipped out of the cell. After checking that the door was locked behind him, Batman hustled down the corridors and out of the asylum. The Batmobile waited for him in the shadows.

The orange glow of the drone's lights enabled Rory to survey his surroundings. Rory had been brought into a storage room of sorts. Drips through the cracked ceiling fed puddles on the cracked floor. Stacks of soggy crates teetered on the verge of collapse. Gimbals of every shape and size—all rusted and unusable, of course—lay in sad piles like an unloved treasure hoard.

As for his floating guardian, its only weaponry seemed to be its laser. Rory knew that laser was far faster than any of his reflexes, yet if he could somehow distract the drone, he might have a chance at disarming it.

"So you're Two-Three-Eight?"

The drone's lights flickered. "Affirmative."

That flickering had lasted for less than a second, but Rory noticed. Since it didn't have the faster AI processor the Elite Drone possessed, it had taken time to process Rory's voice and question.

Perhaps that was the key. If he could get the drone to make computations about its own processor, he would essentially be sending its programming into a loop.

"You do realize you're just a hunk of junk for my uncle to command. He didn't even give you an AI unit for independent thought."

There was another flicker of the drone's lights, a little longer this time. "Independent thought is not necessary. Silence your voice." It waved its laser menacingly.

Rory waited a moment before he spoke again. "What if I said I could replace your processor with a more advanced, artificial intelligence prototype? Would you still want me silenced?"

The twin orange lights flickered—and kept flickering. Its laser tip smoldered red. "Only Elite

Drone One has an AI processor. Other central processors are . . . unavailable. Silence . . ."

"How can I be silent when your computations are wrong?" Rory reached behind him and gripped the Batarang. "See, unknown to your master programmer, when I broke into the lab, I grabbed two processors, not one. I kept the extra in my back pocket."

"Extra processor . . . not used . . . inefficient management of resources . . ."

Rory smiled. "*Very* inefficient. But if you shut off your laser, I can open up your case and swap your processor. Just calculate how much faster and quicker you'll be to do your job, like guarding me."

The drone's lights started to flash many times a second. "Processing speed would increase by incalculable factors . . . upgrade immediately . . . upgrade immediately . . . defense mechanism shutting off . . ."

Rory watched the laser tip slowly fade. After it had gone completely dark, he took the last steps up to the hovering drone, reached past its spinner poles, and opened the case. Drawing the Batarang from his pocket, he cut the wires with its sharp edge, then popped out the processor.

"Should've been happy with what you had, Two-Three-Eight." No longer controlled by its central processor, the spinner blades stopped rotating and the lights dimmed. Rory caught the drone before it dropped into a puddle. Feeling inside the case, he rerouted the wires so that the lights could be powered via the battery. Drone Two-Three-Eight would still be useful as an oversized flashlight.

Having restored the meager illumination, Rory slid the Batarang back into his pocket. He was pondering what to do next when a faint cry sounded from behind a pile of machinery crates. Rory knew who it was even before he looked.

Mom.

CHAPTER 9

Thick ropes bound Rory's mother to a chair. An oily rag muffled her mouth. Her red hair had lost its curl while dirt soiled her skin and blouse. She looked thin and weary, but there was still fight in her eyes.

Rory sliced through the ropes and untied the rag. Her first action was to breathe. Her second was to reach out with weak arms to give her son a hug.

"Rory."

"It's okay, Mom. It's okay."

She was already crying. And in those tears she told him what had happened. She'd escaped the falling buildings of Metropolis, but the trains had stopped running and all the cell towers had been destroyed. She knew she had to get home to Rory, so she did the only thing she could do: walk. On the long journey home, she saw her brother. "I didn't ask how or why he was there. I just was happy to see someone I knew. I even said I was sorry for turning him in. I had been worried.

"He accepted my apology and took me here. Forced me to make his drones. He said if I didn't, he was going to . . . he was going to hurt you."

Rory held her close. "I'm fine, Mom. Don't worry. And I'll get us out of this."

But how? If they went upstairs, even for a peek, there were still nine more drones to worry about. Getting past them was going to be impossible without help.

Then it occurred to Rory that he could get help.

RE-1 was still upstairs. RE-1 could fly somewhere and send a message when they couldn't.

"One minute, Mom." Rory slipped out of his mother's hug. She squeezed his arm, not wanting to let go. He took out the radio control to RE-1 and pro-grammed a command.

The Gotham Gimbals factory was situated in one of the bleakest parts of the city, an urban wasteland of forsaken warehouses and overgrown parking lots. Batman had spent so much time in the area it felt like a second home.

A home he could never fully get clean.

He parked across the street from the factory and reviewed the equipment on his Utility Belt. Bata-rangs, check. Infrared goggles, check. Lock picks, check. Smoke capsule, check. Rebreather, check. He'd brought everything he thought he would need.

Scanning the area for suspicious types, and see-ing no one, he hastened toward the gimbal factory.

A jungle of weeds had sprouted around the rear entrance. Some stalks grew past Batman's waist.

They slowed him down, but also provided extra cover in the night. Batman preferred having the element of surprise in his confrontations. If he had the first move, often it was the only move he needed to make to catch his opponent.

He had to be careful, however. Doctor Aesop was no dumb thug or petty thief. Though Batman's true identity was unknown to him, the fact that he was plotting to take down Bruce Wayne made him extremely dangerous.

Clambering onto the freight dock, Batman found the bay door locked. He unclasped the lock pick kit from his Utility Belt when something nearby buzzed. Batman stood flush against the door. Out of a broken factory window whizzed a drone with a body made of cheap plastic. It bobbed and canted due to damaged spinner blade poles—damage Batman had caused. The drone was the same mechanical apparatus that had been strapped to the back of the boy Rory at WayneTech labs.

Two more drones, these built out of metal, shot out of the window. They fired lasers during their pursuit. The other drone's erratic flying pattern made it a difficult target. But one of the drones spied Batman. "Alert! Intruder! Alert!"

Batman flung a Batarang at the drone, knocking it back through the window where it crashed inside. His next Batarang struck the second drone dead center, slicing it in half. Both chunks fell into the weeds.

With the element of surprise gone, Batman didn't pick the lock of the bay door. He just kicked it down.

"Who do we have here?" said a crazed voice. "Could I have woken up Batman?"

The speaker was none other than Doctor Babrius Aesop. Standing at the other end of the factory, he wore a dirty lab coat and lens-less glasses. About thirty more drones hovered around him. The tips of their protruding lasers glowed brightly.

"Order them to switch off, Aesop," Batman said. "You are ill. I will take you back to Arkham where you will get the help you need."

"You know what kind of help they give? They lock you up in a cell. Padded, so you don't hurt yourself. Then they talk to you. They talk and talk and talk, asking questions, trying to figure out what disturbs you. And I tell them. I tell them the only thing that disturbs me is Bruce Wayne. I tell them I'm the way I am because of the way he and his company cronies treated me. How they stole my ideas and discredited me."

"I heard you wanted to commercialize the technology," Batman said. "Technology that wasn't ready."

"It was ready—and if those buffoons hadn't gotten in the way, I could've made billions! The world would be kneeling before me, Doctor Babrius Aesop, and my drone army."

"Perhaps Mister Wayne did you a favor," Batman said. "Perhaps he saw your madness and stopped you from doing something terrible."

"He only stoked my wrath, Batman. And he will pay. Bruce Wayne will pay."

Batman took up a fighting stance. "You'll have to get past me first, Doctor Aesop."

"I welcome that challenge. My Drone Strike Team needs a quality test." Doctor Aesop stepped behind the drones and made a cutting gesture at Batman. "Elite Drone One, attack this intruder!"

"Affirmative," said the lead drone with the red lights.

In unison, the drones unleashed their lasers. But Batman was too fast. He jumped atop a work-bench and began to leapfrog from bench to bench, hurling Batarangs at the drones. Caught off guard, two more drones met their end. One was propelled into a manufacturing machine, the other sent twirl-ing outside.

The elite drone rotated itself in Batman's direc-tion, needing a moment to recharge its lasers before firing again. This shot singed Batman's cape as he somersaulted in the air. Four more laser beams came at Batman, so close he could feel the heat. He landed on the floor, and rolled, scattering gim-bal casings. He scooped up a bunch of axis rings and flung them at the nearest drone. Instead of fir-ing at Batman, the drone and its companions blasted the rings. One of the machines was destroyed in the cross fire.

This gave Batman precious seconds to run toward Doctor Aesop while the drones' lasers recharged.

Aesop did not flee. He merely chuckled. "You won't evade them forever. They'll wear you down. And when I've built an army of them, I'll throw all the other men like you into Arkham Asylum to wail and wither."

"You're mistaken," Batman said. "There are no other men like me."

He ducked a barrage of lasers and cast three more Batarangs at the drones. Just one hit a target, but it did the work of three. The struck drone flipped and careened into the drone hovering beside it, which in turn did the same to its neighbor. Entangled, their spinner blades bit into each other, cutting through the poles. The three drones collapsed in a heap.

"Do you really want to continue this?" Batman asked.

"Elite Drone One, full fury mode."

"Affirmative."

The drone's blades whirled so fast they became a blur. It darted at Batman, up and down, all around him, shooting short precise beams that didn't require recharging. Batman dived, rolled, and threw Batarang after Batarang. He destroyed a few more drones, but the elite drone was too quick. One of the drone's lasers lanced Batman's leg. Another needled him in the side. A third nailed him in the chest. He fell, whacking a table on his way to the ground. Steel filings needled his suit. This time he did more than wince.

"Thus ends the mighty Batman," Aesop said. "Elite Drone One, finish him."

Batman lifted his head. The elite drone's laser was recharging for a powerful blast. Doctor Aesop was grinning. Out of all the criminals he had apprehended, out of all perilous places from which he had emerged alive, was this how it ended?

Batman would not go out like this. He refused. "Always," Batman muttered, "turn a bad situation . . . into good."

Aesop knitted his brows. "What?"

"The moral of your fable," Batman said, "of the bat and the weasel."

Batman crushed a capsule on his Utility Belt. The world suddenly became one of a dense dark black smoke.

Knockout gas. Aesop took this as his cue to leave. While the remaining drones attacked Batman, he made a run for the storage room. Batman saw the scientist flee. He couldn't stop Aesop while the drones were still firing all around him. But at least he had made it harder for the villain to escape.

CHAPTER 10

Clark felt uneasy departing from the factory. He had come as a journalist, which meant covering a story rather than getting involved in it. Yet what Doctor Aesop had said about the drones, and his treatment of his young nephew, made Clark more than suspicious. It made him *want* to get involved.

Lois probably felt the same at times. But she

always stayed neutral. Her power was in her reporting. She revealed the truth and let others decide what to do. Clark would follow her example. He would be a reporter first and foremost, and Superman only when necessary.

Lights twinkled on the bridge that connected the two cities. He would take the ferry instead of fly. The trip would allow him to clear his mind. He'd get back to Metropolis right on time for a late-night pizza with Lois.

Something buzzed behind him. He turned. Wobbling through the air was what looked like a child's plastic pencil case equipped with miniature helicopter wings—a poor man's drone. Its LEDs flashed a single word in Morse code.

Help.

The signal was all Clark needed to know his work here as a journalist was done. Someone was in danger, probably that boy.

He needed Superman.

The sounds of combat echoed from the factory floor. Though he wanted to see what was going on,

Rory knew he was safest tucked away in the storage room, where he could guard his mother, and wait for RE-1 to bring help.

That might not come soon enough. His mom started to cough, as did he. Smoke was beginning to fill up the storage room. They'd asphyxiate if they inhaled too much of it.

"We need to go," Amelia said, struggling to stand up from her chair.

"Not so fast." His uncle stood in the doorway to the storage room, holding one of the drone's lasers in his hands. "You're going to walk in front of me," he paused to cough, "as my hostages."

"I'd rather die," Rory's mother said.

"That can be arranged, Amelia." Uncle Aesop aimed his laser at her.

"No!" Rory stepped in front of her. "We'll go."

Rory gripped his mom's hand and led her out of the storage room. Uncle Aesop gestured to the window—or where the window should be. Smoke was everywhere, making it impossible to see.

Rory felt along the wall for the edge of the sill. Then he reached up, undoing the clasp and inching the window upward. He pushed harder and felt a blast of cold air as the window slammed open. Black smoke began spilling out around him.

Rory turned back to help his mother out first, his lungs tightening as he tried not to breath in. His head pounded. But he helped her step over the high frame and out into the fresh air. Unable to hold his breath any longer, he ducked his head through the window and dived after her. They both fell into the weeds, gasping.

When he caught his breath, he lifted his head. His uncle stood a few feet away, still brandishing the weapon. "Up, both of you. Let's move. Or you can take your chances with Batman."

"Batman?" Rory glanced at the factory. Smoke billowed out of the windows. "Is Batman in there?"

"I said move!" his uncle shouted.

"Leave them alone," boomed a voice. Striding through the weeds, unaffected by the smoke, was a caped figure. But he wore red and blue instead of black and gray, and no mask cowled his face.

Rory gasped again, and not because of the smoke in his lungs. "Superman."

Uncle Aesop whirled, triggering his laser. The beam shot out, hitting Superman directly in the chest.

Superman shrugged off the blast as if it were a bee sting and continued to walk forward. Alarmed, his uncle turned the laser back on Rory's mom. "Drop it," Superman said.

Uncle Aesop cackled, at the end of his wits. "Only if you leave now and never return. You have three seconds to fly away . . . Two . . ."

Superman slowly walked toward Aesop with his hands outstretched. "This can all end peacefully."

Suddenly, Rory had an idea. He reached into his pocket and pushed the button on RE-1's remote.

"One . . ."

Superman was about to leap into the air when RE-1 swooped down in front of Rory. Its pencil case of a body caught the triggered blast and blew apart, causing Uncle Aesop to drop the weapon. Superman retrieved it and bent it in half as if it was a feather.

Uncle Aesop fumed at Rory. "You little gerbil— he's an alien. He'll kill us all!"

He sprinted into the factory, disappearing in the smoke.

Superman did not pursue and held Rory back from doing the same. "You two need medical attention. Grab my arms. I'll fly you to a hospital."

Rory didn't argue. His mom was in bad shape, and his lungs were on fire. Besides, if Batman was still in the factory, he would take care of his uncle.

And Rory didn't want to miss having a chance to fly with Superman.

That night, Rory and his mother soared through the sky. From that height they could see the cranes scattered throughout Metropolis, rebuilding the broken city. Things were finally going to be normal again.

Though the smoke was thick, Batman never coughed, not once. The rebreather he'd brought on his Utility Belt fit over his nostrils, and filtered the toxins out of the smoke. It did not, however, diminish the pain of his laser burns. The wreckage of twenty-nine drones littered the floor. Now, only the elite drone was left.

Although he could breathe, he was unable to see more than a foot around him. Fortunately, the dense smoke had the same effect on his opponents, mechanical and living. It shrouded Batman from the elite drone's targeting system.

He was out of Batarangs, but his Utility Belt carried one last item of use. A pair of infrared goggles. He unfolded them and stretched them over his eyes. They wouldn't help him see in the visible spectrum, yet they could detect heat that emanated from the human body and machines.

Turning around, Batman glimpsed random beams in the infrared shooting at the ground. The elite drone was still on the attack, though confused at where its target was located.

Approaching, Batman adjusted his position according to the elite drone's chaotic firing pattern, skirting to the right or the left, staying always behind the beam. When he neared within a few feet, he could see the heat of the drone's casing in the air in front of him.

Hooking an arm around Elite Drone One, he grabbed the laser tube and snapped it off.

"Alert, alert! Laser nonoperational! Hostile seizure of Elite Drone One unit! Alert!" Its spinner blades revolved even faster, taking Batman off his feet.

Batman let go, giving the elite drone a mighty shove. It rose so rapidly it smashed into the factory ceiling. The resulting explosion glowed a bright red in his goggles.

In response to the explosion, Batman heard a wail of panic.

Aesop. So the weasel had returned.

Batman crept through the smoke, spotting Aesop's heat signature huddled in a corner. As he approached, the doctor began to cough violently. Whatever had caused him to run back into the factory must have been terrifying enough for the doctor to take his chances with the knockout gas. Coming up behind Aesop, Batman put a hand over the villain's mouth, shackled his wrists, and dragged him out the rear door to the Batmobile. The mad doctor was too weak to offer much resistance.

Before he went off to patrol the streets, Batman made one stop. He dumped Doctor Aesop at Arkham Asylum.

Then he drove away into the dark night.

EPILOGUE

Clark hurried down the street toward Giuseppe's pizzeria. A lone figure waited outside. Her arms were crossed. Her glare stopped him cold. "You're late," Lois Lane said.

"I'm sorry," Clark said. "I got a little tied up."

"It took you five hours to do an interview?

Gotham City's not that far away, even in rush-hour traffic."

"Well . . . it wasn't just an interview."

Her eyes narrowed further. "You got involved, didn't you?"

"I couldn't help myself," Clark said. "A boy and his mother were in danger."

"From who?"

"A scientist named Doctor Aesop, who is actually the boy's uncle. He recently escaped from Arkham and was preparing to build—"

"Let me see your notes."

Clark gave her his notepad. She read it under the light of the streetlamp. "You gotta practice your shorthand. It's atrocious."

"What do you think? I asked some pretty good questions, didn't I?" Clark swayed from side to side. His stomach growled. "I could really go for that pizza right now."

Lois looked up at him. "Are you serious?"

"Lois, I'm not that different. My appetite's the same as everyone else's."

She shook her head. "Is your X-ray vision that bad?"

"What?" He followed her gaze to the pizzeria. A neon sign on the window read CLOSED. "Oh. I am late."

"By like an hour," she said.

He looked about. "There should be a food truck around here."

"We don't have time for that. We'll grab a coffee at the diner. We've got too much work to do to get this in by tomorrow's deadline." She flapped the notepad closed, then walked down the street.

Puzzled, Clark followed. "We? That's my story, Lois!"

She frowned at him. "You going to write about yourself?"

He blanked for a moment, then adjusted his glasses. "I was going to write about Doctor Aesop."

"The story's not about Doctor Aesop. It's about Superman saving a boy and his mother from Doctor Aesop. You said so yourself."

He hesitated. By intervening, he had made Superman the story. He had no regrets about it, though he didn't want to come back to Perry White empty-handed. "Well, what about the interview? Can't we publish that?"

"I'll use it as background. Don't worry, I'll acknowledge your contribution," she said with a wink.

The diner shone ahead. Some insomniacs could be seen sitting at tables through the window. "So you're saying I shouldn't have gotten involved," Clark said.

"Quite the contrary," Lois said. "I think you're a hero. You sacrificed writing the lead article in tomorrow's edition for saving people's lives. I wish I could do that."

"Yeah, but it won't save me from White."

She leaned her back into the door of the diner, opening it. "You still have that blog article to write on the telethon, don't you?"

Clark sighed. Even he would need coffee. It was going to be a long night.

Located in Metropolis, the Hotel Grand Lux subscribed solely to the *Daily Planet*, so that's what the server gave to Bruce Wayne. He sat at a table in the hotel's five-star restaurant, waiting for his lunch date. If Miss Crane, the real estate developer who had won the telethon bid, did not come within the next ten minutes, Bruce was free to go.

To pass the time, Bruce glanced at the head-line of the morning paper, and a smirk came to his lips:

SUPERMAN SAVES BOY AND MOTHER
FROM MAD SCIENTIST

The article by Lois Lane detailed Superman's rescue in Gotham City of Rory and Amelia Greeley from their closest of kin, a fugitive of Arkham Asylum, Doctor Babrius Aesop. Nowhere did the text mention Batman or how he defeated the drones and hauled Doctor Babrius Aesop back to Arkham. The only other name referenced in the article was a credit to "Clark Kent" for additional reporting.

"I'd let it go, Master Wayne," said a voice with a British accent. "You don't do this for publicity."

Bruce lowered the paper. Alfred sat down

across from him. "Looks like Crane canceled, thank goodness."

Alfred gestured for the server to come over. "Might I have some English breakfast tea, with milk? And a menu, too?"

The server went into the kitchen. Bruce folded the paper and dropped it on the table. "You're going to make me sit here while you drink and eat?"

Alfred unveiled a sly smile. "I won't be the full two hours."

Bruce's eyes narrowed. "Don't tell me *you're* Miss Crane?"

"The phone operator may have mistaken my accented miss for mister, but if you remember, Crane is my middle name."

The server returned with tea and a menu. "Cheers," Alfred said.

Bruce stared at Alfred as the gentleman sipped his tea and browsed the menu. "How much did you spend on me?"

"You have your secrets, Master Wayne, and I have mine. But as I mentioned before, it *has* been a while since the two of us lunched," Alfred said. "What better way to arrange it than by assisting those families who suffered so greatly in the attack?"

"You're a good man, Alfred Pennyworth."

"It goes with the company." Alfred held out the menu. "I recommend the paniki stew. It's delicious."

Bruce waved off the menu. "That's what I'll have," he told the server.

The two lunched, enjoying a stay for much longer than two hours.

So many people attended the Metropolis-Gotham City Young Engineers' Challenge that the organizers had to move the event out of the gymnasium into a parking lot. Even then, it was hard to get a glimpse of the action. Students of all ages from both cities demonstrated their technical prowess by showing off what they had designed and built. Among the most applauded projects on display were a battery-operated pet groomer, a lawn sprinkler that used collected rainwater, and an entertainment-exercise

bike that powered a television while the rider ped-
aled away calories.

Rory was nervous that his project didn't match
up with these other projects. But Miss Paiva didn't
seem concerned. And his mother smiled the entire
time. So he stood on the sidelines, watching and
waiting for the inevitable.

"Next up we have Rory Greeley of Lewis Wilson
Middle School!" called a judge. "Come join us in the
ring and strut your stuff, young man!"

Rory took a deep breath, received a pat on his
back from his mom, and then walked out. His project walked with him.

The judge, a lady who was a science teacher
at another school, held out a microphone for Rory
to speak into. "Tell us a little about your project,"
she said.

"Well . . ." The microphone squealed. Rory
winced at the noise. A happy look from his mother
kept him going. "I . . . originally designed a flying
drone. But I ended up working with a friend on a
model that had more personality."

"Does it do any tricks?" the judge asked.

"Arr-Eee-Two, sit," Rory said.

RE-2, a robotic dog cobbled together from a shoebox, a jewelry case, and paper-towel-roll tubes, bent its cardboard legs to squat on the ground. A plastic tongue darted out of its mouth and fake eyeballs rolled around on its head.

"Arr-Eee-Two, come."

The dog raised its legs and waddled over to him.

"So much more obedient than my Chihuahua," the judge said. "Can I trade?"

The audience of parents and students laughed. The dog's internal speaker woofed in response. It wagged its tail.

"Sorry," Rory said. "This model's taken."

Standing beside his mother and Miss Paiva were Ajay, his lunch buddies, Mina, and Ellie. She was looking at Rory and smiling.

Rory wasn't upset when he didn't win a prize that day. He had all he needed.

It was break time at Arkham. The other patients played badminton or cards. Aesop avoided everyone and sat by himself in the yard.

His beard and hair had grown out, and he wore asylum scrubs instead of the lab coat. Since he had destroyed the hard disks with his records, he was forced to undergo a battery of medical and psychological tests again. The doctors had declared him in prime physical health, with no lung damage from the smoke, yet he felt worse than ever. He had been so close to getting his revenge, yet he had failed so utterly. He doubted he would ever get over it.

Jackalope bounded over to him. "Doctor Aesop! You're back!"

He sneered at the button-nosed, buck-toothed, antler-headed lunatic. "Go away."

"Why? You came back for Jack! Now Jack forgives you!" Jackalope bounced from one foot to the other. "Can you tell Jack a story?"

"I'm out of stories."

Jackalope blinked his wide eyes. "You're out of stories?"

"That's what I said."

"Then let me tell you one," Jackalope said. "There once was a bat who was snatched by a weasel . . ."

Aesop buried his head in his hands. The stories that had once been a comfort to him now only reminded him of his failures. And with Jack at his side, he would be reliving those failures over and over for the rest of his life. It seemed that Aesop had been wrong: Not all bad situations turned good.

ABOUT THE AUTHOR

MICHAEL KOGGE's other recent work includes *Empire of the Wolf*, an epic graphic novel featuring werewolves in Rome, and the junior novel adaptation for *Star Wars: The Force Awakens*, along with the Star Wars Rebels series of chapter books. He resides online at MichaelKogge.com, while his real home is located in Los Angeles.